Our Little German Cousin

Mary Hazelton Blanchard Wade

Our Little German Cousin

CHAPTER I
CHRISTMAS

"Don't look! There, now it's done!" cried Bertha.

It was two nights before Christmas. Bertha was in the big living-room with her mother and older sister. Each sat as close as possible to the candle-light, and was busily working on something in her lap.

But, strange to say, they did not face each other. They were sitting back to back.

"What an unsociable way to work," we think. "Is that the way Germans spend the evenings together?"

No, indeed. But Christmas was near at hand, and the air was brimful of secrets.

Bertha would not let her mother discover what she was working for her, for all the world. And the little girl's mother was preparing surprises for each of the children. All together, the greatest fun of the year was getting ready for Christmas.

"Mother, you will make some of those lovely cakes this year, won't you?" asked Bertha's sister Gretchen.

"Certainly, my child. It would not be Christmas without them. Early to-morrow morning, you and Bertha must shell and chop the nuts. I will use the freshest eggs and will beat the dough as long as my arms will let me."

"Did you always know how to make those cakes, mamma?" asked Bertha.

"My good mother taught me when I was about your age, my dear. You may watch me to-morrow, and perhaps you will learn how to make them. It is never too early to begin to learn to cook."

"When the city girls get through school, they go away from home and study housekeeping don't they?" asked Gretchen.

"Yes, and many girls who don't live in cities. But I hardly think you will ever be sent away. We are busy people here in our little village, and you will have to be contented with learning what your mother can teach you.

"I shall be satisfied with that, I know. But listen! I can hear father and Hans coming."

"Then put up your work, children, and set the supper-table."

The girls jumped up and hurriedly put the presents away. It did not take long to set the supper-table, for the meals in this little home were very simple, and supper was the simplest of all. A large plate of black bread and a pitcher of sour milk were brought by the mother, and the family gathered around the table.

The bread wasn't really black, of course. It was dark brown and very coarse. It was made of rye meal. Bertha and Gretchen had never seen any white bread in their lives, for they had never yet been far away from their own little village. Neither had their brother Hans.

They were happy, healthy children. They all had blue eyes, rosy cheeks, and fair hair, like their father and mother.

"You don't know what I've got for you, Hans," said Bertha, laughing and showing a sweet little dimple in her chin.

Hans bent down and kissed her. He never could resist that dimple, and Bertha was his favourite sister.

"I don't know what it is, but I do know that it must be something nice," said her brother.

When the supper-table had been cleared, the mother and girls took out their sewing again, while Hans worked at some wood-carving. The father took an old violin from its case and began to play some of the beautiful airs of Germany.

When he came to the "Watch on the Rhine," the mother's work dropped from her hands as she and the children joined in the song that stirs every German heart.

"Oh, dear! it seems as though Christmas Eve never would come," sighed Bertha, as she settled herself for sleep beside her sister.

It was quite a cold night, but they were cosy and warm. Why shouldn't they be? They were covered with a down feather bed. Their mother had the same kind of cover on her own bed, and so had Hans.

But Christmas Eve did come at last, although it seemed so far off to Bertha the night before. Hans and his father brought in the bough of a yew-tree, and it was set up in the living-room.

The decorating came next. Tiny candles were fastened on all the twigs. Sweetmeats and nuts were hung from the branches.

"How beautiful! How beautiful!" exclaimed the children when it was all trimmed, and they walked around it with admiring eyes.

None of the presents were placed on the tree, for that is not the fashion in Germany. Each little gift had been tied up in paper and marked with the name of the one for whom it was intended.

When everything was ready, there was a moment of quiet while the candles were being lighted. Then Bertha's father began to give out the presents, and there was a great deal of laughing and joking as the bundles were opened.

There was a new red skirt for Bertha. Her mother had made it, for she knew the child was fond of pretty dresses. Besides this, she had a pair of warm woollen mittens which Gretchen had knit for her. Hans had made and carved a doll's cradle for each of the girls.

Everybody was happy and contented. They sang songs and cracked nuts and ate the Christmas cakes to their hearts' content.

"I think I like the ones shaped like gnomes the best," said Hans. "They have such comical little faces. Do you know, every time I go out in the forest, it seems as though I might meet a party of gnomes hunting for gold."

"I like the animal cakes best," said Bertha. "The deer are such graceful creatures, and I like to bite off the horns and legs, one at a time."

"A long time ago," said their father, "they used to celebrate Christmas a little different from the way we now do. The presents were all carried to a man in the village who dressed himself in a white robe, and a big wig made of flax. He covered his face with a mask, and then went from house to house. The grown people received him with great honours. He called for the children and gave them the presents their parents had brought to him.

"But these presents were all given according to the way the children had behaved during the year. If they had been good and tried hard, they had the gifts they deserved. But if they had been naughty and disobedient, it was not a happy time for them."

"I don't believe the children were very fond of him," cried Hans. "They must have been too much afraid of him."

"That is true," said his father. "But now, let us play some games. Christmas comes but once a year, and you have all been good children."

The room soon rang with the shouts of Hans and his sisters. They played "Blind Man's Buff" and other games. Their father took part in all of them as though he were a boy again. The good mother looked on with pleasant smiles.

Bedtime came only too soon. But just before the children said good night, the father took Hans one side and talked seriously yet lovingly with him. He told the boy of the faults he must still fight against. He spoke also of the improvement he had made during the year.

At the same time the mother gave words of kind advice to her little daughters. She told them to keep up good courage; to be busy and patient in the year to come.

"My dear little girls," she whispered, as she kissed them, "I love to see you happy in your play. But the good Lord who cares for us has given us all some work to do in this world. Be faithful in doing yours."

"Wake up, Bertha. Come, Gretchen. You will have to hurry, for it is quite late," called their mother. It was one morning about a week after Christmas.

man and woman
BERTHA'S FATHER AND MOTHER.
"Oh dear, I am so sleepy, and my bed is nice and warm," thought Bertha.

But she jumped up and rubbed her eyes and began to dress, without waiting to be called a second time. Her mother was kind and loving, but she had taught her children to obey without a question.

Both little girls had long, thick hair. It must be combed and brushed and braided with great care. Each one helped the other. They were soon dressed, and ran down-stairs.

As soon as the breakfast was over and the room made tidy, every one in the family sat down to work. Bertha's father was a toy-maker. He had made wooden images of Santa Claus all his life. His wife and children helped him.

When Bertha was only five years old, she began to carve the legs of these Santa Claus dolls. It was a queer sight to see the little girl's chubby fingers at their work. Now that she was nine years old, she still carved legs for Santa Claus in her spare moments.

Gretchen always made arms, while Hans worked on a still different part of the bodies. The father and mother carved the heads and finished the little images that afterward gave such delight to children in other lands.

Bertha lives in the Black Forest. That name makes you think at once of a dark and gloomy place. The woods on the hills are dark, to be sure, but the valleys nestling between are bright and cheerful when the sun shines down and pours its light upon them.

Bertha's village is in just such a valley. The church stands on the slope above the little homes. It seems to say, "Look upward, my children, to the blue heavens, and do not fear, even when the mists fill the valley and the storm is raging over your heads."

All the people in the village seem happy and contented. They work hard, and their pay is small, but there are no beggars among them.

Toys are made in almost every house. Every one in a family works on the same kind of toy, just as it is in Bertha's home.

The people think: "It would be foolish to spend one's time in learning new things. The longer a person works at making one kind of toy, the faster he can make them, and he can earn more money."

One of Bertha's neighbours makes nothing but Noah's Arks. Another makes toy tables, and still another dolls' chairs.

Bertha often visits a little friend who helps her father make cuckoo-clocks. Did you ever see one of these curious clocks? As each hour comes around, a little bird comes outside the case. Then it flaps its wings and sings "cuckoo" in a soft, sweet voice as many times as there are strokes to the hour. It is great fun to watch for the little bird and hear its soft notes.

Perhaps you wonder what makes the bird come out at just the right time. It is done by certain machinery inside the clock. But, however it is, old people as well as children seem to enjoy the cuckoo-clocks of Germany.

"Some day, when you are older, you shall go to the fair at Easter time," Bertha's father has promised her.

"Is that at Leipsic, where our Santa Claus images go?" asked his little daughter.

"Yes, my dear, and toys from many other parts of our country. There you will see music-boxes and dolls' pianos and carts and trumpets and engines and ships. These all come from the mining-towns.

"But I know what my little Bertha would care for most. She would best like to see the beautiful wax dolls that come from Sonneberg."

"Yes, indeed," cried Bertha. "The dear, lovely dollies with yellow hair like mine. I would love every one of them. I wish I could go to Sonneberg just to see the dolls."

"I wonder what makes the wax stick on," said Gretchen, who came into the room while her father and Bertha were talking.

"After the heads have been moulded into shape, they are dipped into pans of boiling wax," her father told her. "The cheap dolls are dipped only once, but the expensive ones have several baths before they are finished. The more wax that is put on, the handsomer the dolls are.

"Then comes the painting. One girl does nothing but paint the lips. Another one does the cheeks. Still another, the eyebrows. Even then Miss Dolly looks like a bald-headed baby till her wig is fastened in its place."

"I like the yellow hair best," said Bertha. "But it isn't real, is it, papa?"

"I suppose you mean to ask, 'Did it ever grow on people's heads?' my dear. No. It is the wool of a kind of goat. But the black hair is real hair. Most dolls, however, wear light wigs. People usually prefer them."

"Do little girls in Sonneberg help make the dolls, just as Bertha and I help you on the Santa Claus images?" asked Gretchen.

"Certainly. They fill the bodies with sawdust, and do other easy things. But they go to school, too, just as you and Bertha do. Lessons must not be slighted."

"If I had to help make dolls, just as I do these images," said Gretchen to her sister as their father went out and left the children together, "I don't believe I'd care for the handsomest one in the whole toy fair. I'd be sick of the very sight of them."

"Look at the time, Bertha. See, we must stop our work and start for school," exclaimed Gretchen.

It was only seven o'clock in the morning, but school would begin in half an hour. These little German girls had to study longer and harder than their

American cousins. They spent at least an hour a day more in their schoolrooms.

As they trudged along the road, they passed a little stream which came trickling down the hillside.

"I wonder if there is any story about that brook," said Bertha. "There's a story about almost everything in our dear old country, I'm sure."

"You have heard father tell about the stream flowing down the side of the Kandel, haven't you?" asked Gretchen.

"Yes, I think so. But I don't remember it very well. What is the story, Gretchen?"

"You know the Kandel is one of the highest peaks in the Black Forest. You've seen it, Bertha."

"Yes, of course, but tell the story, Gretchen."

"Well, then, once upon a time there was a poor little boy who had no father or mother. He had to tend cattle on the side of the Kandel. At that time there was a deep lake at the summit of the mountain. But the lake had no outlet.

"The people who lived in the valley below often said, 'Dear me! how glad we should be if we could only have plenty of fresh water. But no stream flows near us. If we could only bring some of the water down from the lake!'

"They were afraid, however, to make a channel out of the lake. The water might rush down with such force as to destroy their village. They feared to disturb it.

"Now, it came to pass that the Evil One had it in his heart to destroy these people. He thought he could do it very easily if the rocky wall on the side of the lake could be broken down. There was only one way in which this could be done. An innocent boy must be found and got to do it.

"It was a long time before such an one could be found. But at last the Evil One came across an orphan boy who tended cattle on the mountainside. The poor little fellow was on his way home. He was feeling very sad, for he was thinking of his ragged clothes and his scant food.

"'Ah ha!' cried the Evil One to himself, 'here is the very boy.'

"He changed himself at once so he had the form and dress of a hunter, and stepped up to the lad with a pleasant smile.

"'Poor little fellow! What is the matter? And what can I do for you?' he said, in his most winning manner.

"The boy thought he had found a friend, and told his story.

"'Do not grieve any longer. There is plenty of gold and silver in these very mountains. I will show you how to become rich,' said the Evil One. 'Meet me here early to-morrow morning and bring a good strong team with you. I will help you get the gold.'

"The boy went home with a glad heart. You may be sure he did not oversleep the next morning. Before it was light, he had harnessed four oxen belonging to his master, and started for the summit of the mountain.

"The hunter, who was waiting for him, had already fastened a metal ring around the wall that held in the waters of the lake.

"'Fasten the oxen to that ring,' commanded the hunter, 'and the rock will split open.'

"Somehow or other, the boy did not feel pleased at what he was told to do. Yet he obeyed, and started the oxen. But as he did so, he cried, 'Do this in the name of God!'

"At that very instant the sky grew black as night, the thunder rolled and the lightning flashed. And not only this, for at the same time the mountain shook and rumbled as though a mighty force were tearing it apart."

"What became of the poor boy?" asked Bertha.

"He fell senseless to the ground, while the oxen in their fright rushed headlong down the mountainside. But you needn't get excited, Bertha, no harm was done. The boy was saved as well as the village, because he had pulled in the name of God.

"The rock did not split entirely. It broke apart just enough to let out a tiny stream of water, which began to flow down the mountainside.

"When the boy came to his senses, the sky was clear and beautiful once more. The sun was shining brightly, and the hunter was nowhere to be seen. But the stream of water was running down the mountainside.

"A few minutes afterward, the boy's master came hurrying up the slope. He was frightened by the dreadful sounds he had heard. But when he saw the waterfall, he was filled with delight.

"'Every one in the village will rejoice,' he exclaimed, 'for now we shall never want for water.'

"Then the little boy took courage and told the story of his meeting the hunter and what he had done.

"'It is well you did it in the name of the Lord,' cried his master. 'If you had not, our village would have been destroyed, and every one of us would have been drowned.'"

"See! the children are going into the schoolhouse, Gretchen. We must not be late. Let's run," said Bertha.

The two little girls stopped talking, and hurried so fast that they entered the schoolhouse and were sitting in their seats in good order before the schoolmaster struck his bell.

CHAPTER III
THE WICKED BISHOP

"The Rhine is the loveliest river in the world. I know it must be," said Bertha.

"Of course it is," answered her brother. "I've seen it, and I ought to know. And father thinks so, too. He says it is not only beautiful, but it is also bound into the whole history of our country. Think of the battles that have been fought on its shores, and the great generals who have crossed it!"

"Yes, and the castles, Hans! Think of the legends father and mother have told us about the beautiful princesses who have lived in the castles, and the brave knights who have fought for them! I shall be perfectly happy if I can ever sail down the Rhine and see the noted places on its shores."

"The schoolmaster has taught you all about the war with France, hasn't he, Bertha?"

"Of course. And it really seemed at one time as if France would make us Germans agree to have the Rhine divide the two countries. Just as if we would be willing to let the French own one shore of our beautiful river. I should say not!"

Bertha's cheeks grew rosier than usual at the thought of such a thing. She talked faster than German children usually do, for they are rather slow in their speech.

"We do not own all of the river, little sister, as it is. The baby Rhine sleeps in an icy cradle in the mountains of Switzerland. Then it makes its way through our country, but before it reaches the sea it flows through the low lands of Holland."

"I know all that, Hans. But we own the best of the Rhine, anyway. I am perfectly satisfied."

"I wish I knew all the legends about the river. There are enough of them to fill many books. Did you ever hear about the Rats' Tower opposite the town of Bingen, Bertha?"

"What a funny name for a tower! No. Is there a story about it, Hans?"

"Yes, one of the boys was telling it to me yesterday while we were getting wood in the forest. It is a good story, although my friend said he wasn't sure it is true."

"What is the story?"

"It is about a very wicked bishop who was a miser. It happened one time that the harvests were poor and grain was scarce. The cruel bishop bought all the grain he could get and locked it up. He intended to sell it for a high price, and in this way to become very rich.

"As the days went by, the food became scarcer and scarcer. The people began to sicken and die of hunger. They had but one thought: they must get something to eat for their children and themselves.

"They knew of the stores of grain held by the bishop. They went to him and begged for some of it, but he paid no attention to their prayers. Then they demanded that he open the doors of the storehouse and let them have the grain. It was of no use.

"At last, they gathered together, and said:

"'We will break down the door if you do not give it to us.'

"'Come to-morrow,' answered the bishop. 'Bring your friends with you. You shall have all the grain you desire.'

"The morrow came. Crowds gathered in front of the granary. The bishop unlocked the door, saying:

"'Go inside and help yourselves freely.'

"The people rushed in. Then what do you think the cruel bishop did? He ordered his servants to lock the door and set the place on fire!

"The air was soon filled with the screams of the burning people. But the bishop only laughed and danced. He said to his servants:

"'Do you hear the rats squeaking inside the granary?'

"The next day came. There were only ashes in place of the great storehouse. There seemed to be no life about the town, for the people were all dead.

"Suddenly there was a great scurrying, as a tremendous swarm of rats came rushing out of the ashes. On they came, more and more of them. They filled the streets, and even made their way into the palace.

"The wicked bishop was filled with fear. He fled from the place and hurried away over the fields. But the swarm of rats came rushing after him. He came to Bingen, where he hoped to be safe within its walls. Somehow or other, the rats made their way inside.

Tower next to a fiver
THE RATS' TOWER.
"There was now only one hope of safety. The bishop fled to a tower standing in the middle of the Rhine. But it was of no use! The rats swam the river and made their way up the sides of the tower. Their sharp teeth gnawed holes through the doors and windows. They entered in and came to the room where the bishop was hiding."

"Wicked fellow! They killed and ate him as he deserved, didn't they?" asked Bertha.

"There wasn't much left of him in a few minutes. But the tower still stands, and you can see it if you ever go to Bingen, although it is a crumbling old pile now."

"Rats' Tower is a good name for it. But I would rather hear about enchanted princesses and brave knights than wicked old bishops. Tell me another story, Hans."

"Oh, I can't. Listen! I hear some one coming. Who can it be?"

Hans jumped up and ran to the door, just in time to meet his Uncle Fritz, who lived in Strasburg.

The children loved him dearly. He was a young man about twenty-one years old. He came home to this little village in the Black Forest only about once a year. He had so much to tell and was so kind and cheerful, every one was glad to see him.

"Uncle Fritz! Uncle Fritz! We are so glad you've come," exclaimed Bertha, putting her arms around his neck. "And we are going to have something that you like for dinner."

"I can guess what it is. Sauerkraut and boiled pork. There is no other sauerkraut in Germany as good as that your mother makes, I do believe. I'm hungry enough to eat the whole dishful and not leave any for you children. Now what do you say to my coming? Don't you wish I had stayed in Strasburg?"

"Oh, no, no, Uncle Fritz. We would rather see you than anybody else," cried Hans. "And here comes mother. She will be just as glad as we are."

That evening, after Hans had shown his uncle around the village, and he had called on his old friends, he settled himself in the chimney-corner with the children about him.

"Talk to us about Strasburg, Uncle Fritz," begged Gretchen.

"Please tell us about the storks," said Bertha. "Are there great numbers of the birds in the city, and do they build their nests on the chimneys?"

"Yes, you can see plenty of storks flying overhead if you will come back with me," said Uncle Fritz, laughingly. "They seem to know the people love them. If a stork makes his home about any one's house, it is a sign of good fortune to the people who live there.

"'It will surely come,' they say to themselves, 'and the storks will bring it.' Do you wonder the people like the birds so much?"

"I read a story about a mother stork," said Bertha, thoughtfully. "She had a family of baby birds. They were not big enough to leave their nest, when a fire broke out in the chimney where it was built. Poor mother bird! She could have saved herself. But she would not leave her babies. So she stayed with them and they were all burned to death together."

"I know the story. That happened right in Strasburg," said her uncle.

"Please tell us about the beautiful cathedral with its tall tower," said Hans. "Sometime, uncle, I am going to Strasburg, if I have to walk there, and then I shall want to spend a whole day in front of the wonderful clock."

"You'd better have a lunch with you, Hans, and then you will not get hungry. But really, my dear little nephew, I hope the time will soon come when you can pay me a long visit. As for the clock, you will have to stay in front of it all night as well as all day, if you are to see all it can show you."

"I know about cuckoo-clocks, of course," said Gretchen, "but the little bird is the only figure that comes out on those. There are ever so many different figures on the Strasburg clock, aren't there, Uncle Fritz?"

"A great, great many. Angels strike the hours. A different god or goddess appears for each day in the week. Then, at noon and at midnight, Jesus and his twelve apostles come out through a door and march about on a platform.

"You can imagine what the size of the clock must be when I tell you that the figures are as large as people. When the procession of the apostles appears, a gilded cock on the top of the tower flaps its wings and crows.

"I cannot begin to tell you all about it. It is as good as a play, and, as I told Hans, he would have to stay many hours near it to see all the sights."

"I should think a strong man would be needed to wind it up," said his nephew.

"The best part of it is that it does not need to be wound every day," replied Uncle Fritz. "They say it will run for years without being touched. Of course, travellers are coming to Strasburg all the time. They wish to see the clock, but they also come to see the cathedral itself. It is a very grand building, and, as you know, the spire is the tallest one in all Europe.

"Then there is so much beautiful carving! And there are such fine statues. Oh, children, you must certainly come to Strasburg before long and see the cathedral of which all Germany is so proud."

"Strasburg was for a time the home of our greatest poet," said Bertha. "I want to go there to see where he lived."

The child was very fond of poetry, even though she was a little country girl. Her father had a book containing some of Goethe's ballads, and she loved to lie under the trees in the pleasant summer-time and repeat some of these poems.

"They are just like music," she would say to herself.

"A marble slab has been set up in the old Fish Market to mark the spot where Goethe lived," said Uncle Fritz. "They say he loved the grand cathedral of the city, and it helped him to become a great writer when he was a young student there. I suppose its beauty awakened his own beautiful thoughts."

The children became quiet as they thought of their country and the men who had made her so strong and great,—the poets, and the musicians, and the brave soldiers who had defended her from her enemies.

Uncle Fritz was the first one to speak.

"I will tell you a story of Strasburg," he said. "It is about something that happened there a long time ago. You know, the city isn't on the Rhine itself, but it is on a little stream flowing into the greater river.

"Well, once upon a time the people of Zurich, in Switzerland, asked the people of Strasburg to join with them in a bond of friendship. Each should help the other in times of danger. The people of Strasburg did not think much of the idea. They said among themselves: 'What good can the little town of Zurich do us? And, besides, it is too far away.' So they sent back word that they did not care to make such a bond. They were scarcely polite in their message, either.

"When they heard the reply, the men of Zurich were quite angry. They were almost ready to fight. But the youngest one of their councillors said:

"'We will force them to eat their own words. Indeed, they shall be made to give us a different answer. And it will come soon, too, if you will only leave the matter with me.'

"'Do as you please,' said the other councillors. They went back to their own houses, while the young man hurried home, rushed out into the kitchen and picked out the largest kettle there.

"'Wife, cook as much oatmeal as this pot will hold,' he commanded.

"The woman wondered what in the world her husband could be thinking of. But she lost no time in guessing. She ordered her servants to make a big fire, while she herself stirred and cooked the great kettleful of oatmeal.

"In the meanwhile, her husband hurried down to the pier, and got his swiftest boat ready for a trip down the river. Then he gathered the best rowers in the town.

"'Come with me,' he said to two of them, when everything had been made ready for a trip. They hastened home with him, as he commanded.

"'Is the oatmeal ready?' he cried, rushing breathless into the kitchen.

"His wife had just finished her work. The men lifted the kettle from the fire and ran with it to the waiting boat. It was placed in the stern and the oarsmen sprang to their places.

"'Pull, men! Pull with all the strength you have, and we will go to Strasburg in time to show those stupid people that, if it should be necessary, we live near enough to them to give them a hot supper.'

"How the men worked! They rowed as they had never rowed before.

"They passed one village after another. Still they moved onward without stopping, till they found themselves at the pier of Strasburg.

"The councillor jumped out of the boat, telling two of his men to follow with the great pot of oatmeal. He led the way to the council-house, where he burst in with his strange present.

"'I bring you a warm answer to your cold words,' he told the surprised councillors. He spoke truly, for the pot was still steaming. How amused they all were!

"'What a clever fellow he is,' they said among themselves. 'Surely we will agree to make the bond with Zurich, if it holds many men like him.'

"The bond was quickly signed and then, with laughter and good-will, the councillors gathered around the kettle with spoons and ate every bit of the oatmeal.

"'It is excellent,' they all cried. And indeed it was still hot enough to burn the mouths of those who were not careful."

"Good! Good!" cried the children, and they laughed heartily, even though it was a joke against their own people.

Their father and mother had also listened to the story and enjoyed it as much as the children.

"Another story, please, dear Uncle Fritz," they begged.

But their father pointed to the clock. "Too late, too late, my dears," he said. "If you sit up any longer, your mother will have to call you more than once in the morning. So, away to your beds, every one of you."

CHAPTER IV
THE COFFEE-PARTY

"How would you like to be a wood-cutter, Hans?"

"I think it would be great sport. I like to hear the thud of the axe as it comes down on the trunk. Then it is always an exciting time as the tree begins to bend and fall to the ground. Somehow, it seems like a person. I can't help pitying it, either."

Hans had come over to the next village on an errand for his father. A big sawmill had been built on the side of the stream, and all the men in the place were kept busy cutting down trees in the Black Forest, or working in the sawmill.

After the logs had been cut the right length, they were bound into rafts, and floated down the little stream to the Rhine.

"The rafts themselves seem alive," said Hans to his friend. "You men know just how to bind the logs together with those willow bands, so they twist and turn about like living creatures as they move down the stream."

"I have travelled on a raft all the way from here to Cologne," answered the wood-cutter. "The one who steers must be skilful, for he needs to be very careful. You know the rafts grow larger all the time, don't you, Hans?"

"Oh, yes. As the river becomes wider, the smaller ones are bound together. But is it true that the men sometimes take their families along with them?"

"Certainly. They set up tents, or little huts, on the rafts, so their wives and children can have a comfortable place to eat and sleep. Then, too, if it rains, they can be sheltered from the storm."

"I'd like to go with you sometime. You pass close to Strasburg, and I could stop and visit Uncle Fritz. Wouldn't it be fun!"

"Hans! Hans!" called a girl's voice just then.

"I don't see her, but I know that's Bertha. She came over to the village with me this afternoon. One of her friends has a coffee-party and she invited us to it. So, good-bye."

"Good-bye, my lad. Come and see me again. Perhaps I can manage sometime to take you with me on a trip down the river."

"Thank you ever so much."

Hans hurried away, and was soon entering the house of a little friend who was celebrating her birthday with a coffee-party.

There were several other children there. They were all dressed in their best clothes and looked very neat and nice. The boys wore long trousers and straight jackets. They looked like little old men. The girls had bright-coloured skirts and their white waists were fresh and stiff.

Their shoes were coarse and heavy, and made a good deal of noise as the children played the different games. But they were all so plump and rosy, it was good to look at them.

"They are a pretty sight," said one of the neighbours, as she poured out the coffee.

"They deserve to have a good time," said another woman with a kind, motherly face. "They will soon grow up, and then they will have to work hard to get a living."

The coffee and cakes were a great treat to these village children. They did not get such a feast every day in the year. Their mothers made cakes only for festivals and holidays, and coffee was seldom seen on their tables oftener than once a week.

In the great cities and fine castles, where the rich people of Germany had their homes, they could eat sweet dainties and drink coffee as often as they liked. But in the villages of the Black Forest, it was quite different.

"Good night, good night," said Hans and Bertha, as they left their friends and trudged off on a path through the woods. It was the shortest way home, and they knew their mother must be looking for them by this time.

It was just sunset, but the children could not see the beautiful colours of the evening sky, after they had gone a short distance into the thick woods.

"Do you suppose there are any bears around?" whispered Bertha.

The trees looked very black. It seemed to the little girl as though she kept seeing the shadow of some big animal hiding behind them.

"No, indeed," answered Hans, quite scornfully. "Too many people go along this path for bears to be willing to stay around here. You would have to go farther up into the forest to find them. But look quickly, Bertha. Do you see that rabbit jumping along? Isn't he a big fellow?"

"See! Hans, he has noticed us. There he goes as fast as his legs can carry him."

By this time, the children had reached the top of a hill. The trees grew very thick and close. On one side a torrent came rushing down over the rocks and stones. It seemed to say:

"I cannot stop for any one. But come with me, come with me, and I will take you to the beautiful Rhine. I will show you the way to pretty bridges, and great stone castles, and rare old cities. Oh, this is a wonderful world, and you children of the Black Forest have a great deal to see yet."

"I love to listen to running water," said Bertha. "It always has a story to tell us."

"Do you see that light over there, away off in the distance?" asked Hans. "It comes from a charcoal-pit. I can hear the voices of the men at their work."

"I shouldn't like to stay out in the dark woods all the time and make charcoal," answered his sister. "I should get lonesome and long for the sunlight."

"It isn't very easy work, either," said Hans. "After the trees have been cut down, the pits have to be made with the greatest care, and the wood must be burned just so slowly to change it into charcoal. I once spent a day in the forest with some charcoal-burners. They told such good stories that night came before I had thought of it."

"I can see the village ahead of us," said Bertha, joyfully.

A few minutes afterward, the children were running up the stone steps of their own home.

"We had such a good time," Hans told his mother, while Bertha went to Gretchen and gave her some cakes she had brought her from the coffee-party.

"I'm so sorry you couldn't go," she told her sister.

"Perhaps I can next time," answered Gretchen. "But, of course, we could not all leave mother when she had so much work to do. So I just kept busy and tried to forget all about it."

"You dear, good Gretchen! I'm going to try to be as patient and helpful as you are," said Bertha, kissing her sister.

CHAPTER V
THE BEAUTIFUL CASTLE

"Father's coming, father's coming," cried Bertha, as she ran down the steps and out into the street.

Her father had been away for two days, and Hans had gone with him. They had been to Heidelberg. Bertha and Gretchen had never yet visited that city, although it was not more than twenty miles away.

"Oh, dear, I don't know where to begin," Hans told the girls that evening.

"Of course, I liked to watch the students better than anything else. The town seems full of them. They all study in the university, of course, but they are on the streets a good deal. They seem to have a fine time of it. Every one carries a small cane with a button on the end of it. They wear their little caps down over their foreheads on one side."

"What colour do they have for their caps, Hans?" asked Gretchen.

"All colours, I believe. Some are red, some blue, some yellow, some green. Oh, I can't tell you how many different kinds there are. But they were bright and pretty, and made the streets look as though it must be a festival day."

"I have heard that the students fight a good many duels. Is that so, Hans?"

"If you should see them, you would certainly think so. Many of the fellows are real handsome, but their faces are scarred more often than not.

"'The more scars I can show, the braver people will think I am.' That is what the students seem to think. They get up duels with each other on the smallest excuse. When they fight, they always try to strike the face. Father says their duelling is good practice. It really helps to make them brave. If I were a student, I should want to fight duels, too."

Bertha shuddered. Duelling was quite the fashion in German universities, but the little girl was very tender-hearted. She could not bear to think of her brother having his face cut up by the sword of any one in the world.

"What do you think, girls?" Hans went on. "Father had to go to the part of the town nearest the castle. He said he should be busy for several hours, and I could do what I liked. So I climbed up the hill to the castle, and wandered all around it. I saw a number of English and American people there. I suppose they had come to Heidelberg on purpose to see those buildings.

"'Isn't it beautiful!' I heard them exclaim again and again. And I saw a boy about my own age writing things about it in a note-book. He told his mother he was going to say it was the most beautiful ruin in Germany. He was an American boy, but he spoke our language. I suppose he was just learning it, for he made ever so many mistakes. I could hardly tell what he was trying to say."

"What did his mother answer?" asked Bertha.

"She nodded her head, and then pointed out some of the finest carvings and statues. But she and her son moved away from me before long, and then I found myself near some children of our country. They must have been rich, for they were dressed quite grandly. Their governess was with them. She told them to notice how many different kinds of buildings there were, some of them richly carved, and some quite plain. 'You will find here palaces, towers, and fortresses, all together,' she said. 'For, in the old days, it was not only a grand home, but it was also a strong fortress.'"

people in a courtyard
COURTYARD OF HEIDELBERG CASTLE.
"You know father told us it was not built all at once," said Gretchen. "Different parts were added during four hundred years."

"Yes, and he said it had been stormed by the enemy, and burned and plundered," added Bertha. "It has been in the hands of those horrid Frenchmen several different times. Did you see the blown-up tower, Hans?"

"Of course I did. Half of it, you know, fell into the moat during one of the sieges, but linden-trees have grown about it, and it makes a shady nook in which to rest one's self."

"You did not go inside of the castle, did you, Hans?" asked Gretchen.

"No. It looked so big and gloomy, I stayed outside in the pretty gardens. I climbed over some of the moss-grown stairs, though, and I kept discovering something I hadn't seen before. Here and there were old fountains and marble statues, all gray with age."

"They say that under the castle are great, dark dungeons," said Bertha, shivering at the thought.

"What would a castle be without dungeons?" replied her brother. "Of course there are dungeons. And there are also hidden, underground passages through which the people inside could escape in times of war and siege."

"Oh, Hans! did you see the Heidelberg Tun?" asked Gretchen.

Now, the Heidelberg Tun is the largest wine-cask in the whole world. People say that it holds forty-nine thousand gallons. Just think of it! But it has not been filled for more than a hundred years.

"No, I didn't see it," replied Hans. "It is down in the cellar, and I didn't want to go there without father. I heard some of the visitors telling about the marks of the Frenchmen's hatchets on its sides. One of the times they captured the castle, they tried to break open the tun. They thought it was full of wine. But they did not succeed in hacking through its tough sides."

"Good! Good!" cried his sisters. They had little love for France and her people.

That evening, after Hans had finished telling the girls about his visit, their father told them the legend of Count Frederick, a brave and daring man who once lived in Heidelberg Castle.

Count Frederick was so brave and successful that he was called "Frederick the Victorious."

Once upon a time he was attacked by the knights and bishops of the Rhine, who had banded together against him. When he found what great numbers of soldiers were attacking his castle, Count Frederick was not frightened in the least. He armed his men with sharp daggers, and marched boldly out against his foes.

They attacked the horses first of all. The daggers made short work, and the knights were soon brought to the ground. Their armour was so heavy that it was an easy matter then to make them prisoners and take them into the castle.

But Frederick treated them most kindly. He ordered a great banquet to be prepared, and invited his prisoners to gather around the board, where all sorts of good things were served.

One thing only was lacking. There was no bread. The guests thought it was because the servants had forgotten it, and one of them dared to ask for a piece. Count Frederick at once turned toward his steward and ordered the bread to be brought. Now his master had privately talked with the steward and had told him what words to use at this time.

"I am very sorry," said the steward, "but there is no bread."

"You must bake some at once," ordered his master.

"But we have no flour," was the answer.

"You must grind some, then," was the command.

"We cannot do so, for we have no grain."

"Then see that some is threshed immediately."

"That is impossible, for the harvests have been burned down," replied the steward.

"You can at least sow grain, that we may have new harvests as soon as possible."

"We cannot even do that, for our enemies have burned down all the buildings where the grain was stored for seed-time."

Frederick now turned to his visitors, and told them they must eat their meat without bread. But that was not all. He told them they must give him enough money to build new houses and barns to take the places of those they had destroyed, and also to buy new seed for grain.

"It is wrong," he said, sternly, "to carry on war against those who are helpless, and to take away their seeds and tools from the poor peasants."

It was a sensible speech. It made the knights ashamed of the way they had been carrying on war in the country, and they left the castle wiser and better men.

All this happened long, long ago, before Germany could be called one country, for the different parts of the land were ruled over by different people and in different ways.

This same Count Frederick, their father told them, had great love for the poor. When he was still quite young, he made a vow. He said, "I will never marry a woman of noble family."

Not long after this, he fell in love with a princess. But he could not ask her to marry him on account of the vow he had made.

He was so unhappy that he went into the army. He did not wish to live, and hoped he would soon meet death.

But the fair princess loved Frederick as deeply as he loved her, and as soon as she learned of the vow he had made, she made up her mind what to do.

She put on the dress of a poor singing-girl, and left her grand home. She followed Frederick from place to place. They met face to face one beautiful evening. Then it was that the princess told her lover she had given up her rank and title for his sake.

How joyful she made him as he listened to her story! You may be sure they were soon married, and the young couple went to live in Heidelberg Castle, where they were as happy and as merry as the day is long.

CHAPTER VI
THE GREAT FREDERICK

"I declare, Hans, I should think you would get tired of playing war," said Bertha. She was sitting under the trees rocking her doll. She was playing it was a baby.

Hans had just come home after an afternoon of sport with his boy friends. But all they had done, Bertha declared, was to play war and soldiers. She had watched them from her own yard.

"Tired of it! What a silly idea, Bertha. It won't be many years before I shall be a real soldier. Just picture me then! I shall have a uniform, and march to music. I don't know where I may go, either. Who knows to what part of the world the emperor will send his soldiers at that time?"

"I know where you would like to go in our own country," said Bertha.

"To Berlin, of course. What a grand city it must be! Father has been there. Our schoolmaster was there while he served his time as a soldier. At this very moment, it almost seems as though I could hear the jingling of the officers' swords as they move along the streets. The regiments are drilled every day, and I don't know how often the soldiers have sham battles."

Hans jumped up from his seat under the tree and began to march up and down as though he were a soldier already.

"Attention, battalion! Forward, march!" Bertha called after him. But she was laughing as she spoke. She could not help it, Hans looked so serious. At the same time she couldn't help envying her brother a little, and wishing she were a boy, too. It must be so grand to be a soldier and be ready to fight for the emperor who ruled over her country.

crowd around statue of manon horse
STATUE OF FREDERICK THE GREAT.
"The schoolmaster told us boys yesterday about the grand palace at Berlin. The emperor lives in it when he is in the city," said Hans, wheeling around suddenly and stopping in front of Bertha.

"I think you must have caught my thoughts," said the little girl, "for the emperor was in my mind when you began to speak."

"Well, never mind that. Do you wish to hear about the palace?"

"Of course I do, Hans."

"The schoolmaster says it has six hundred rooms. Just think of it! And one of them, called the White Room, is furnished so grandly that ,, marks were spent on it. You can't imagine it, Bertha, of course. I can't, either."

A German mark is worth about twenty-four cents of American money, so the furnishing of the room Hans spoke of must have cost about $,. It was a large sum, and it is no wonder the boy said he could hardly imagine so much money.

"There are hundreds of halls in the palace," Hans went on. "Some of their walls are painted and others are hung with elegant silk draperies. The floors are polished so they shine like mirrors. Then the pictures and the armour, Bertha! It almost seemed as though I were there while the schoolmaster was describing them."

"I never expect to see such lovely things," said his sober little sister. "But perhaps I shall go to Berlin some day, Hans. Then I can see the statue of Frederick the Great, at any rate."

"It stands opposite the palace," said her brother, "and cost more than any other bronze statue in the world."

"How did you learn that, Hans?"

"The schoolmaster told us so. He said, too, that it ought to stir the blood of every true German to look at it. There the great Frederick sits on horseback, wearing the robe in which he was crowned, and looking out from under his cocked hat with his bright, sharp eyes. That statue alone is enough to make the soldiers who march past it ready to give their lives for their country."

"He lived when the different kingdoms were separated from each other, and there was no one ruler over all of them. I know that," said Bertha.

"Yes, he was the King of Prussia. And he fought the Seven Years' War with France and came out victorious. Hardly any one thought he could succeed, for there was so much against him. But he was brave and determined. Those two things were worth everything else."

"That wasn't the only war he won, either, Hans."

"No, but it must have been the greatest. Did you know, Bertha, that he was unhappy when he was young? His father was so strict that he tried to run away from Germany with two of his friends. The king found out what they meant to do. One of the friends was put to death, and the other managed to escape."

"What did his father do to Frederick?" Bertha's eyes were full of pity for a prince who was so unhappy as to wish to run away.

"The king ordered his son to be put to death. But I suppose he was angry at the time, for he changed his mind before the sentence was carried out, and forgave him."

"I wonder how kings and emperors live," said Bertha, slowly. It seemed as though everything must be different with them from what it was with other people.

"I'll tell you about Frederick, if you wish to listen."

"Of course I do, Hans."

"In the first place, he didn't care anything about fine clothes, even if he was a king and was born in the grand palace at Berlin. His coat was often very shabby.

"In the next place, he slept only about four hours out of the whole twenty-four for a good many years. He got up at three o'clock on summer mornings, and in the winter-time he was always dressed by five, at the very latest.

"While his hair-dresser was at work, he opened his most important letters. After that, he attended to other business affairs of the country. These things were done before eating or drinking. But when they had been attended to, the king went into his writing-room and drank a number of glasses of cold water. As he wrote, he sipped coffee and ate a little fruit from time to time.

"He loved music very dearly, and sometimes rested from his work and played on his flute.

"Dinner was the only regular meal of the day. It was served at twelve o'clock, and lasted three or four hours. There was a bill of fare, and the names of the cooks were given as well as the dishes they prepared."

"Did the king ever let them know whether he was pleased or not with their cooking?" asked Bertha.

"Yes. He marked the dishes he liked best with a cross. He enjoyed his dinner, and generally had a number of friends to eat with him. There was much joking, and there were many clever speeches.

"When the meal was over, the king played on his flute a short time, and then attended to more business."

"Did he work till bedtime, Hans?"

"Oh, no. In the evening there was a concert or lecture, or something like that. But, all the same, the king was a hardworking man, even in times of peace."

"He loved his people dearly, father once told me," said Bertha. "He said he understood his subjects and they understood him."

"Yes, and that reminds me of a story the schoolmaster told. King Frederick was once riding through the street when he saw a crowd of people gathered together. He said to his groom, 'Go and see what is the matter.' The man came back and told the king that the people were all looking at a caricature of Frederick himself. A caricature, you know, is a comical portrait.

"Perhaps you think the king was angry when he heard this. Not at all. He said, 'Go and hang the picture lower down, so they will not have to stretch their necks to see it.'

"The crowd heard the words. 'Hurrah for the king!' they cried. At the same time, they began to tear the picture into pieces."

"Frederick the Great could appreciate a joke," said Bertha. "I should think the people must have loved him."

"He had some fine buildings put up in his lifetime," Hans went on. "A new palace was built in Berlin, besides another one the king called 'Sans Souci.' Those are French words meaning, 'Without a Care.' He called the place by that name because he said he was free-hearted and untroubled while he stayed there.

"I've told you these things because you are a girl. But I'll tell you what I like to think of best of all. It's the stories of the wars in which he fought and in which he showed such wonderful courage. So, hurrah for Frederick the Great, King of Prussia!"

Hans made a salute as though he stood in the presence of the great king. Then he started for the wood-pile, where he was soon sawing logs with as much energy as if he were fighting against the enemies of his country.

CHAPTER VII
THE BRAVE PRINCESS

"Listen, children! That must be the song of a nightingale. How sweet it is!"

It was a lovely Sunday afternoon. Every one in the family had been to church in the morning, and come home to a good dinner of bean soup and potato salad. Then the father had said:

"Let us take a long walk over the fields and through the woods. The world is beautiful to-day. We can enjoy it best by leaving the house behind us."

Some of the neighbours joined the merry party. The men smoked their pipes, while the women chatted together and the children frolicked about them and picked wild flowers.

How many sweet smells there were in the fields! How gaily the birds sang! The air seemed full of peace and joy.

They all wandered on till they came to a cascade flowing down over some high rocks. Trees grew close to the waterfall, and bent over it as though to hide it from curious eyes. It was a pretty spot.

"Let us sit down at the foot of this cascade," said Bertha's father. "It is a pleasant place to rest."

Every one liked the plan. Bertha nestled close to her father's side.

"Tell us a story. Please do," she said.

"Ask neighbour Abel. He knows many a legend of just such places as this. He has lived in the Hartz Mountains, and they are filled with fairy stories."

The rest of the party heard what was said.

"Neighbour Abel! A story, a story," they cried.

Of course the kind-hearted German could not refuse such a general request. Besides, he liked to tell stories. Taking his long pipe out of his mouth, he laid it down on the ground beside him. Then he cleared his throat and began to speak.

"Look above you, friends. Do you see that mark on the rocky platform overhead? I noticed it as soon as I got here. It made me think of a wild spot in the Hartz Mountains where there is just such a mark. The people call it 'The Horse's Hoof-print.' I will tell you how they explain its coming there.

"Once upon a time there was a beautiful princess. Her name was Brunhilda, and she lived in Bohemia. She lived a gay and happy life, like most young princesses, till one day a handsome prince arrived at her father's palace. He was the son of the king of the Hartz country.

"Of course, you can all guess what happened. The prince fell in love with the princess, and she returned his love. The day was set for the wedding, and the young prince went home to prepare for the great event.

"But he had been gone only a short time when a powerful giant arrived at Brunhilda's home. He came from the far north. His name was Bodo.

"He asked for the princess in marriage, but her heart had already been given away. She did not care for the giant, even though he gave her the most elegant presents,—a beautiful white horse, jewels set in gold, and chains of amber.

"'I dare not refuse the giant,' said Brunhilda's father. 'He is very powerful, and we must not make him angry. You must marry him, my daughter, in three days.'

"The poor maiden wept bitterly. It seemed as though her heart would break. But she was a clever girl, and she soon dried her tears and began to think of some plan by which she might yet be free. She began to smile upon the giant and treat him with great kindness.

"'I should like to try the beautiful horse you brought me,' she said to him. He was much pleased. The horse was brought to the door. The princess mounted him and rode for a time up and down in front of the palace.

"The very next day was that set apart for the wedding. The castle was filled with guests who feasted and made merry. The giant entered into everything with a will. He laughed till the floors and walls shook. Little did he think what was taking place. For the princess slipped out of the castle when no one was watching, hurried into the stable, and leaped upon the back of her swift white horse.

"'Lower the drawbridge instantly,' she called to the guard. She passed over it, and away she flew like the wind.

"You were too late, too late, O giant, when you discovered that Brunhilda was missing.

"He flew out of the castle, and on the back of his own fiery black horse he dashed after the runaway princess.

"On they went! On, on, without stopping. Over the plains, up and down the hillsides, through the villages. The sun set and darkness fell upon the world, but there was never a moment's rest for the maiden on the white horse or the giant lover on his black steed.

"Sometimes in the darkness sparks were struck off from the horses' hoofs as they passed over rough and rocky places. These sparks always showed the princess ahead and slowly increasing the distance between herself and her pursuer.

"When the morning light first appeared, the maiden could see the summit of the Brocken ahead of her. It was the home of her lover. Her heart leaped within her. If she could only reach it she would be safe.

"But alas! her horse suddenly stood still. He would not move. He had reached the edge of a precipice. There it lay, separating the princess from love and safety.

"The brave girl had not a moment to lose. The giant was fast drawing near. She wheeled her horse around; then, striking his sides a sharp blow with her whip, she urged him to leap across the precipice.

"The spring must be strong and sure. It was a matter of life and death. The chasm was deep. If the horse should fail to strike the other side securely, it meant a horrible end to beast and rider.

"But he did not fail. The feet of the brave steed came firmly down upon the rocky platform. So heavily did they fall that the imprint of a hoof was left upon the rock.

"The princess was now safe. It would be an easy matter for her to reach her lover's side.

"As for the giant, he tried to follow Brunhilda across the chasm. But he was too heavy and his horse failed to reach the mark. The two sank together to the bottom of the precipice."

Every one thanked the story-teller, and begged him to tell more of the Hartz Mountains, where he had spent his boyhood days. The children were delighted when he spoke of the gnomes, in whom he believed when he was a child.

"Every time I went out in the dark woods," he said, "I was on the lookout for these funny little fairies of the underground world. I wanted to see them, but at the same time I was afraid I should meet them.

"I remember one time that my mother sent me on an errand through the woods at twilight. I was in the thickest part of the woods, when I heard a sound that sent a shiver down my back.

"'It is a witch, or some other dreadful being,' I said to myself. 'Nothing else could make a sound like that.' My teeth chattered. My legs shook so, I could hardly move. Somehow or other, I managed to keep on. It seemed as though hours passed before I saw the lights of the village. Yet I suppose it was not more than fifteen minutes.

"When I was once more safe inside my own home, I told my father and mother about my fright.

"'It was no witch, my child,' said my father. 'The sound you describe was probably the cry of a wildcat. I thank Heaven that you are safe. A wildcat is not a very pleasant creature to meet in a lonely place.'

"After that, I was never sent away from the village after dark.

"My boy friends and I often came across badgers and deer, and sometimes foxes made their way into the village in search of poultry, but I never came nearer to meeting a wildcat than the time of which I have just told you."

"What work did you do out of school hours?" asked Hans. The boy was thinking of the toys he had to carve.

"My mother raised canary-birds, and I used to help her a great deal. Nearly every woman in the village was busy at the same work. What concerts we did have in those days! Mother tended every young bird she raised with the greatest care. Would it become a good singer and bring a fair price? We waited anxiously for the first notes, and then watched to see how the voices gained in strength and sweetness.

"It was a pleasant life, and I was very happy among the birds in our little village. Would you like to hear a song I used to sing at that time? It is all about the birds and bees and flowers."

"Do sing it for us," cried every one.

Herr Abel had a good voice and they listened with pleasure to his song. This is the first stanza:

"I have been on the mountain
That the song-birds love best.
They were sitting, were flitting,
They were building their nest.
They were sitting, were flitting,
They were building their nest."
After he had finished, he told about the mines in which some of his friends worked. It was a hard life, with no bright sunlight to cheer the men in those deep, dark caverns underground.

"Of course you all know that the deepest mine in the world is in the Hartz Mountains."

His friends nodded their heads, while Hans whispered to Bertha, "I should like to go down in that mine just for the sake of saying I have been as far into the earth as any living person."

"The sun is setting, and there is a chill in the air," said Bertha's father. "Let us go home."

CHAPTER VIII
WHAT THE WAVES BRING

man and boy with house in background

BERTHA'S HOME.

Bertha's mother had just come in from a hard morning's work in the fields. She had been helping her husband weed the garden.

She spent a great deal of time outdoors in the summer-time, as many German peasant women do. They do a large share of the work in ploughing the grain-fields and harvesting the crops. They are much stronger than their American cousins.

"Supper is all ready and waiting for you," said Bertha.

The little girl had prepared a dish of sweet fruit soup which her mother had taught her to make.

"It is very good," said her father when he had tasted it. "My little Bertha is getting to be quite a housekeeper."

"Indeed, it is very good," said her mother. "You learned your lesson well, my child."

Bertha was quite abashed by so much praise. She looked down upon her plate and did not lift her eyes again till Gretchen began to tell of a new amber bracelet which had just been given to one of the neighbours.

"It is beautiful," said Gretchen, quite excitedly. "The beads are such a clear, lovely yellow. They look so pretty on Frau Braun's neck, I don't wonder she is greatly pleased with her present."

"Who sent it to her?" asked her mother.

"Her brother in Cologne. He is doing well at his trade, and so he bought this necklace at a fair and sent it to his sister as a remembrance. He wrote her a letter all about the sights in Cologne, and asked Frau Braun to come and visit him and his wife.

"He promised her in the letter that if she would come, he would take her to see the grand Cologne cathedral. He said thousands of strangers visit it every year, because every one knows it is one of the most beautiful buildings in all Europe.

"Then he said she should also see the Church of Saint Ursula, where the bones of the eleven thousand maidens can still be seen in their glass cases."

"Do you know the story of St. Ursula, Gretchen?" asked her father.

"Yes, indeed, sir. Ursula was the daughter of an English king. She was about to be married, but she said that before the wedding she would go to Rome on a pilgrimage.

"Eleven thousand young girls went with the princess. On her way home she was married, but when the wedding party had got as far as Cologne, they were attacked by the savage Huns. Every one was killed,—Ursula, her husband, and the eleven thousand maidens. The church was afterward built in her memory. Ursula was made a saint by the Pope, and the bones of the young girls were preserved in glass cases in the church."

"Did Frau Braun tell of anything else her brother wrote?" asked her mother.

"He spoke of the bridge of boats across the river, and said she would enjoy watching it open and shut to let the steamers and big rafts pass through. And he told of the Cologne water that is sold in so many of the shops. It is hard to tell which makes the town most famous, the great cathedral or the Cologne water."

"Father, how was the bridge of boats made?" asked Bertha.

"The boats were moored in a line across the river. Planks were then laid across the tops and fastened upon them. Vessels cannot pass under a bridge of this kind, so it has to be opened from time to time. They say it is always interesting to see this done."

"Yes, Frau Braun said she would rather see the bridge of boats than anything else in the city. She has already begun to plan how she can save up enough money to make the trip."

"I will go over there to-morrow to see he new necklace," said Bertha. "But what is amber, father?"

"If you should go to the northern part of Germany, Bertha, you would see great numbers of men, women, and children, busy on the shores of the ocean. The work is greatest in the rough days of autumn, when a strong wind is blowing from the northeast.

"Then the men dress themselves as though they were going out into a storm. They arm themselves with nets and plunge into the waves, which are bringing treasure to the shore. It is the beautiful amber we admire so much.

"The women and children are waiting on the sands, and as the men bring in their nets, the contents are given into their hands. They separate the precious lumps of amber from the weeds to which they are clinging."

Their father stopped to fill his pipe, and the children thought he had come to the end of the story.

"But you haven't told us yet what amber is," said Bertha.

"Be patient, my little one, and you shall hear," replied her father, patting her head. "As yet, I have not half told the story. But I will answer your question at once.

"A long time ago, longer than you can imagine, Bertha, forests were growing along the shores of the Baltic Sea. There was a great deal of gum in the trees of these forests. It oozed out of the trees in the same manner as gum from the spruce-tree and resin from the pine.

"Storms arose, and beds of sand and clay drifted over the forests. They were buried away for thousands of years, it may be. But the motion of the sea washes up pieces of the gum, which is of light weight.

"The gum has become changed while buried in the earth such a long, long time. Wise men use the word 'fossilized' when they speak of what has happened to it. The now beautiful, changed gum is called amber.

"There are different ways of getting it. I told you how it comes drifting in on the waves when the winds are high and the water is rough. But on the pleasant summer days, when the sea is smooth and calm, the men go out a little way from the shore in boats. They float about, looking earnestly over the sides of the boats to the bottom of the sea.

"All at once, they see something. Down go their long hooks through the water. A moment afterward, they begin to tow a tangle of stones and seaweed to the shore. As soon as they land, they begin to sort out the great mass. Perhaps they will rejoice in finding large pieces of amber in the collection.

"There is still another way of getting amber. I know Hans will be most interested in what I am going to say now. It has more of danger in it, and boys like to hear anything in the way of adventure."

Hans looked up and smiled. His father knew him well. He was a daring lad. He was always longing for the time when he should grow up and be a soldier, and possibly take part in some war.

"Children," their father went on, "you have all heard of divers and of their dangerous work under the sea. Gretchen was telling me the other day about her geography lesson, and of the pearl-divers along the shores of India. I did not tell her then that some men spend their lives diving for amber on the shores of our own country.

"They wear rubber suits and helmets and air-chests of sheet iron."

"How can they see where they are going?" asked Bertha.

"There are glass openings in their helmets, and they can look through these. They go out in boats. The crew generally consists of six men. Two of them are divers, and four men have charge of the air-pumps. These pumps force fresh air down through tubes fastened to the helmet of each diver. Besides these men there is an overseer who has charge of everything.

"Sometimes the divers stay for hours on the bed of the sea, and work away at the amber tangles."

"But suppose anything happens to the air-tubes and the men fail to get as much air as they need?" said Hans. "Is there any way of letting those in the boat know they are in trouble? And, besides that, how do the others know when it is time to raise the divers with their precious loads?"

"There is a safety-rope reaching from the boat to the men. When they pull this rope it is a sign that they wish to be drawn up. But I have told you as much about amber now as you will be able to remember."

"Are you very tired, father dear?" said Bertha, in her most coaxing tone.

"Why should I be tired? What do you wish to ask me? Come, speak out plainly, little one."

"You tell such lovely fairy-tales, papa, I was just wishing for one. See! The moon is just rising above the tree-tops. It is the very time for stories of the wonderful beings."

Her father smiled. "It shall be as you wish, Bertha. It is hard to refuse you when you look at me that way. Come, children, let us sit in the doorway. Goodwife, put down your work and join us while I tell the story of Siegfried, the old hero of Germany."

CHAPTER IX
THE MAGIC SWORD

Far away in the long ago there lived a mighty king with his goodwife and his brave son, Siegfried. Their home was at Xanten, where the river Rhine flows lazily along.

The young prince was carefully taught. But when his education was nearly finished, his father said:

"Siegfried, there is a mighty smith named Mimer. It will be well for you to learn all you can of him in regard to the making of arms."

So Siegfried went to work at the trade of a smith. It was not long before he excelled his teacher. This pleased Mimer, who spent many spare hours with his pupil, telling him stories of the olden times.

After awhile, he took Siegfried into his confidence. He said:

"There is a powerful knight in Burgundy who has challenged every smith of my country to make a weapon strong enough to pierce his coat of mail.

"I long to try," Mimer went on, "but I am now old and have not strength enough to use the heavy hammer."

At these words Siegfried jumped up in great excitement.

"I will make the sword, dear master," he cried. "Be of good cheer. It shall be strong enough to cut the knight's armour in two."

Early the next morning, Siegfried began his work. For seven days and seven nights the constant ringing of his hammer could be heard. At the end of that time Siegfried came to his master with a sword of the finest steel in his right hand.

Mimer looked it all over. He then held it in a stream of running water in which he had thrown a fine thread. The water carried the thread against the edge of the sword, where it was cut in two.

"It is without a fault," cried Mimer with delight.

"I can do better than that," answered Siegfried, and he took the sword and broke it into pieces.

Again he set to work. For seven more days and seven more nights he was busy at his forge. At the end of that time he brought a polished sword to his master.

Mimer looked it over with the greatest care and made ready to test it.

He threw the fleeces of twelve sheep into the stream. The current carried them on its bosom to Siegfried's sword. Instantly, each piece was divided as it met the blade. Mimer shouted aloud in his joy.

"Balmung" (for that was the name Siegfried gave the sword) "is the finest weapon man ever made," he cried.

Siegfried was now prepared to meet the proud knight of Burgundy.

The very first thrust of the sword, Balmung, did the work. The head and shoulders of the giant were severed from the rest of the body. They rolled down the hillside and fell into the Rhine, where they can be seen even now, when the water is clear. At least, so runs the story. The trunk remained on the hilltop and was turned to stone.

Soon after this Mimer found that Siegfried longed to see the world and make himself famous. So he bound the sword Balmung to the young prince's side, and told him to seek a certain person, who would give him a fine war-horse.

Siegfried went to this man, from whom he obtained a matchless steed. In fact it had descended from the great god Odin's magic horse. Siegfried, you can see, must have lived in a time when men believed in gods and other wonderful beings.

He was now all ready for his adventures, but before starting out, Mimer told him of a great treasure of gold guarded by a fearful serpent. This treasure was spread out over a plain called the Glittering Heath. No man had yet been able to take it, because of its terrible guardian.

Siegfried was not in the least frightened by the stories he heard of the monster. He started out on his dangerous errand with a heart full of courage.

At last, he drew near the plain. He could see it on the other side of the Rhine, from the hilltop where he was standing. With no one to help him, not even taking his magic horse with him, he hurried down the hillside and sprang into a boat on the shore.

An old man had charge of the boat, and as he rowed Siegfried across, he gave him good advice. This old man, as it happened, was the god Odin, who loved Siegfried and wished to see him succeed.

"Dig a deep trench along the path the serpent has worn on his way to the river when in search of water," said the old boatman. "Hide yourself in the trench, and, as the serpent passes along, you must thrust your sword deep into his body."

It was good advice. Siegfried did as Odin directed him. He went to work on the trench at once. It was soon finished, and then the young prince, sword in hand, was lying in watch for the dread monster.

He did not have long to wait. He soon heard the sound of rolling stones. Then came a loud hiss, and immediately afterward he felt the serpent's fiery breath on his cheek.

And now the serpent rolled over into the ditch, and Siegfried was covered by the folds of his huge body. He did not fear or falter. He thrust Balmung, his wonderful sword, deep into the monster's body. The blood poured forth in such torrents that the ditch began to fill fast.

It was a time of great danger for Siegfried. He would have been drowned if the serpent in his death-agony had not rolled over on one side and given him a chance to free himself.

In a moment more he was standing, safe and sound, by the side of the ditch. His bath in the serpent's blood had given him a great blessing. Hereafter it would be impossible for any one to wound him except in one tiny place on his shoulder. A leaf had fallen on this spot, and the blood had not touched it.

"What did Siegfried do with the golden treasure?" asked Hans, when his father had reached this point in the story.

"He had not sought it for himself, but for Mimer's sake. All he cared for was the power of killing the serpent."

As soon as this was done, Mimer drew near and showed himself ungrateful and untrue. He was so afraid Siegfried would claim some of the treasure that he secretly drew Balmung from out the serpent's body, and made ready to thrust it into Siegfried.

But at that very moment his foot slipped in the monster's blood, and he fell upon the sword and was instantly killed.

Siegfried was filled with horror when he saw what had happened. He sprang upon his horse's back and fled as fast as possible from the dreadful scene.

"What happened to Siegfried after that? Did he have any more adventures?" asked Bertha.

"Yes, indeed. There were enough to fill a book. But there is one in particular you girls would like to hear. It is about a beautiful princess whom he freed from a spell which had been cast upon her."

"What was her name, papa?" asked Gretchen.

"Brunhild, the Queen of Isenland. She had been stung by the thorn of sleep."

Odin, the great god, had said, "Brunhild shall not awake till some hero is brave enough to fight his way through the flames which shall constantly surround the palace. He must then go to the side of the sleeping maiden and break the charm by a kiss upon her forehead."

When Siegfried, in his wanderings, heard the story of Brunhild, he said, "I will make my way through the flames and will myself rescue the fair princess."

He leaped upon the back of his magic steed, and together they fought their way through the fire that surrounded the palace of the sleeping beauty. He reached the gates in safety. There was no sign of life about the place. Every one was wrapped in a deep sleep.

Siegfried made his way to the room of the enchanted princess. Ah! there she lay, still and beautiful, with no knowledge of what was going on around her.

The young knight knelt by her side. Leaning over her, he pressed a kiss upon her forehead. She moved slightly; then, opening her blue eyes, she smiled sweetly upon her deliverer.

At the same moment every one else in the palace woke up and went on with whatever had been interrupted when sleep overcame them.

Siegfried remained for six months with the fair Brunhild and her court. Every day was given up to music and feasting, games and songs. Time passed like a beautiful dream. No one knows how long the young knight might have enjoyed this happy life if Odin had not sent two birds, Thought and Memory, to remind him there were other things for him yet to do.

He did not stop to bid Brunhild farewell, but leaped upon his horse's back and rode away in search of new adventures.

"Dear me, children," exclaimed their father, looking at the clock, "it is long past the time you should be in your soft, warm beds."

"Papa, do you know what day to-morrow is?" whispered Bertha, as she kissed him good night.

"My darling child's birthday. It is ten years to-morrow since your eyes first looked upon the sunlight. They have been ten happy years to us all, though our lives are full of work. What do you say to that, my little one?"

"Very happy, papa dear. You and mother are so kind! I ought to be good as well as happy."

"She is a faithful child," said her mother, after Bertha had left the room. "That is why I have a little surprise ready for to-morrow. I have baked a large birthday cake and shall ask her little friends to share it with her.

"Her aunt has finished the new dress I bought for her, and I have made two white aprons, besides. She will be a happy child when she sees her presents."

The mother closed her eyes and made a silent prayer to the All-Father that Bertha's life should be as joyful as her tenth birthday gave promise of being.

THE END